Mr Pepper's PERFECT PET SHOP

WRITTEN AND ILLUSTRATED BY

ERICA JANE WATERS

meadowside
CHILDREN'S BOOKS

It was the morning of Molly's birthday and she was very, very excited.

She jumped out of bed, put on her best birthday dress and her best birthday shoes, and ran downstairs.

Mummy and Daddy were taking Molly in to town for a special birthday treat.

Molly was thinking of
all the wonderful things
she could choose from...
...sweeties
...ice-cream
...a new toy.
But, "Oh no!"
The toy shop was
closed. So was the
sweety shop and so was
the ice-cream parlour.

Every shop was closed.
"Oh well," said Dad.
"Let's go home."
"Wait," said Molly,
"What's that?"

DO NOT SHAKE

Snaggles

Snaggles

A little bell
tinkled above
the door as Molly
stepped in to the
pet shop. At first it
seemed no-one was
around. But, suddenly,
a cheerful voice spoke
from way up high.

"Mr Pepper at your humble
service. Welcome to my most
perfect pet shop!"

GROW
- YOUR OWN -
GOBLIN

"A PET SHOP!"

declared Molly.
"What a perfect treat a pet
would be. Something I could
love and something that
would love me."

"A pet!" pronounced
Mr Pepper excitedly.
"We have every peculiar
pet possible...

...let me show you

...my favourites."

"We have mouseycorns...

and goblins in a jar...

and a dragon in a box."

EGGS
LUCKY DIP   10P

"Do you have any
hamsters?" asked
Molly.

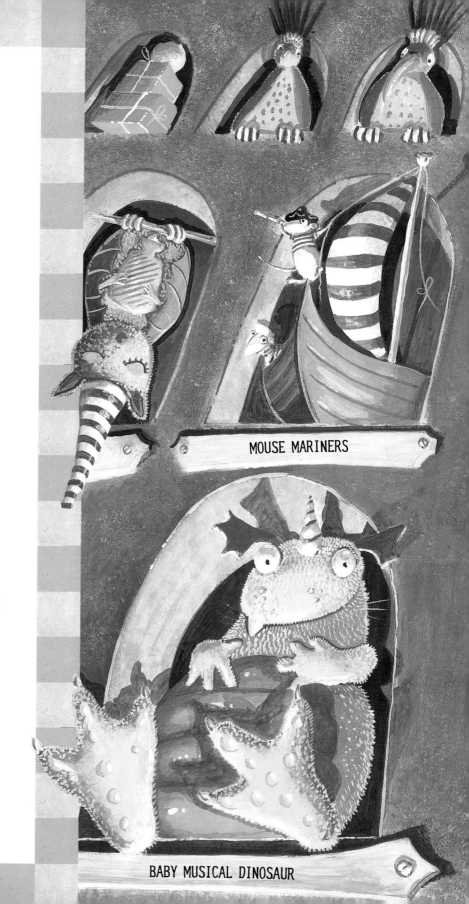

MOUSE MARINERS

BABY MUSICAL DINOSAUR

USEICORNS

GOBLINS IN A JAR (VARIOUS)

CUTE C

ZEBRACORN

DRAGON IN-A-BOX

CAUTION HOT

"I'm afraid not...
I do have some
Mouse Mariners..."

"Too splishy splashy,"
said Molly.

"What about a musical
baby dinosaur"?

DINO BYTES

MONSTER CHUNKS

TREE TRUNK CHUNK
DINO CHUM
—FOR THE HERBIVORE—

"Too noisy!"
shouted Molly.

Pet collars
(with bells)
Various sizes
50P

"Well... how could you resist a baby Zebracorn?"

"Too clippety cloppety,"
said Molly.

"A cute little dragon?"

"Too smokey,"
said Molly.

"Dancing ants?"
"Too small," said Molly.

"A fantastic
flipping frog?"
"Too flippity-floppety"
said Molly.

"A talking penguin?"
"Too chatty,"
said Molly.

List of
things to
chat about
today

1- Sausages
2- Clothes Pegs
3 - Broccoli
4- Pencils

"A Bavarian
bedtime bat?"

"Too sleepy..."
said Molly.

"Well I'm afraid I only
have one thing left...

But, I have no idea
what it is...

All it does is lick your
hand and chase sticks."

"A perfect puppy... I love it. I'll take him!" said Molly.

K-9 GIGANTICUS (PUPPY)
(Average height when fully grown: 75 metres)

"**A**nother perfectly pleasant
and pleased patron,"
thought Mr Pepper.

For Olivia and Peach.
E.J.W.

First published in 2005
by Meadowside Children's Books
185 Fleet Street, London, EC4A 2HS

Text and illustrations © Erica Jane Waters 2005

The right of Erica Jane Waters to be identified as the
author and illustrator of this work has been
asserted by her in accordance with the Copyright,
Designs and Patents Act, 1988

A CIP catalogue record for this book
is available from the British Library
Printed in U.A.E

10 9 8 7 6 5 4 3 2 1